The Curse Of The Obsidian Heart

Mrigendra Bharti

Published by Sellbrochure Vymish Entertainment, 2024.

THE CURSE OF THE OBSIDIAN HEART

First edition. July 13, 2024.

ISBN: 979-8227774057

Written by Mrigendra Bharti.

Table of Contents

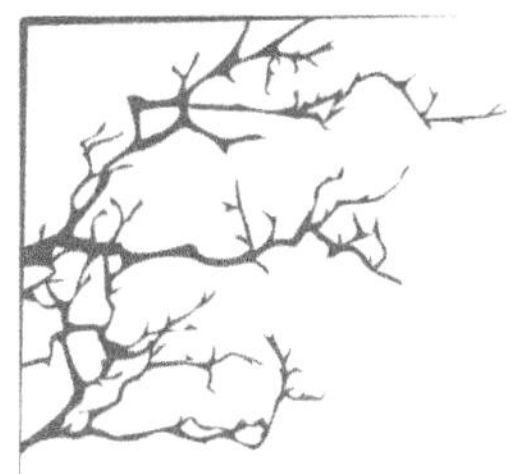

Preface

In the annals of Eldoria, a land bathed in perpetual twilight, whispers of an ancient curse have echoed for generations. It speaks of a heart, not of flesh and blood, but of polished obsidian - a cursed artifact imbued with unimaginable power and darkness. Legend warns of those who dare embrace its touch, for they become forever bound to its chilling embrace.

This tale follows the journey of Seraphina, a young woman ostracized for a darkness that resides within her. When the encroaching shadows of the Shadowbane threaten to consume Eldoria, Seraphina becomes unwittingly entangled with the fabled obsidian heart. Thrust into a destiny she never sought, she must confront not only the monstrous entities of Shadowfell, but also the darkness that resides within herself.

This is a story of courage in the face of fear, of understanding in the face of ignorance, and of a world forced to confront the delicate balance between light and darkness. As Seraphina delves into the heart of Shadowfell, she uncovers a truth that challenges everything Eldoria has held dear. Can she bridge the divide between light and shadow, or will the curse of the obsidian heart consume her and plunge Eldoria into an eternal night?

Prepare to embark on a thrilling adventure where shadows dance and whispers take form. Within these pages, you will encounter valiant warriors, wise counselors, and creatures born from the very essence of darkness. Prepare to be challenged, to be captivated, and to discover the extraordinary power that lies within the embrace of both light and shadow.

WELCOME TO THE WORLD of "The Curse of the Obsidian Heart."

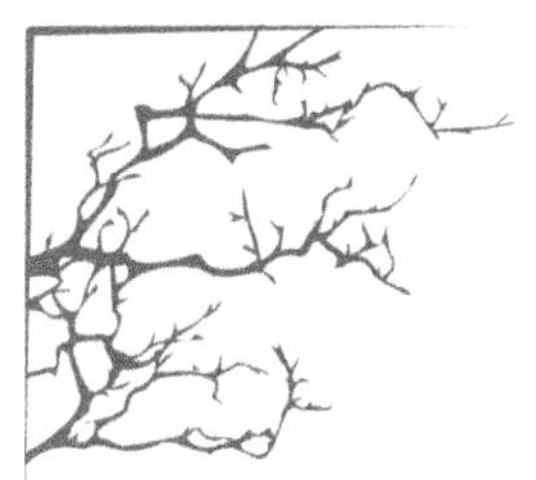

Prologue

The wind howled a mournful dirge as Elara huddled beneath the gnarled branches of the ancient oak. Rain lashed down, each drop a tiny shard of despair reflecting the bleakness that had settled upon Eldoria. For generations, the twilight sun had cast a sickly glow upon the land, its warmth a distant memory.

The whispers, once faint murmurs carried on the night breeze, now shrieked a relentless chorus. They spoke of a creeping darkness, a malevolent force known only as the Shadowbane, that gnawed at the edges of their world. Fear hung heavy in the air, a suffocating shroud that choked all hope.

Elara clutched a worn leather-bound journal, its pages filled with faded script and intricate illustrations. It was the legacy of her grandmother, a revered scholar who had dedicated her life to unraveling the mysteries of the Shadowbane. One particular passage, highlighted with worryingly fresh ink, drew Elara's attention.

"Legend whispers of a hidden power, an artifact forged from the heart of darkness itself - the Obsidian Heart. They say it lies within the uncharted depths of Shadowfell, a treacherous realm where shadows writhe and nightmares take form. Should the wrong soul possess it, the Obsidian Heart could unleash a darkness unimaginable, one that could consume Eldoria in an endless night."

Elara shivered, a cold dread creeping down her spine. The whispers grew louder, almost taunting her. Today, on the cusp of her eighteenth year, a prophecy foretold a chosen one would rise, one marked by a darkness within, destined to either embrace or destroy the Obsidian Heart.

Her heart pounded against her ribs. Her thoughts turned to her childhood friend, Seraphina, a young woman ostracized from their village for the faint shadow that danced in her eyes. Could this be Seraphina's destiny? A tremor of fear shook Elara. She knew Seraphina, her courage, her kindness. But could she face the darkness within, not to mention the horrors of Shadowfell?

As the storm raged on, Elara knew their lives were about to change irrevocably. The curse of the Obsidian Heart cast a long shadow, and Eldoria's fate hung precariously in the balance. Dawn might break, but for Elara, a horrifying truth had been illuminated - the darkness was not just out there, it resided closer than they ever dared imagine.

About Sellbrochure Vymish Entertainment

Sellbrochure Vymish Entertainment, recognized as India's largest book publishing company, has made significant strides in ensuring its extensive collection of books reaches audiences across the global market. This rapid expansion is a testament to the company's dedication to disseminating knowledge and literature far beyond national borders. Central to its success is its affiliation with InkWhirl Media Networks, a reputable entity in the media and publication industry known for its innovative and strategic approaches. Within this network, InkWhirl Publication LLC operates as a vital division, further enhancing the company's capabilities and reach in the international market.

The visionary behind this enterprise is Mrigendra Bharti, the founder of Sellbrochure Vymish Entertainment. His foresight and passion for the literary world have been instrumental in steering the company towards remarkable growth and recognition. Under his leadership, Sellbrochure Vymish Entertainment has not only expanded its catalog but also established a strong presence in both domestic and international markets. Mrigendra Bharti's commitment to excellence and innovation has been a driving force in the company's journey, ensuring that it stays ahead of industry trends and meets the evolving needs of readers worldwide.

Sellbrochure Vymish Entertainment operates under the robust support of its parental organization, Mrigendra Bharti Group InfoTech. This affiliation provides the necessary resources and strategic guidance, enabling the publishing company to undertake ambitious projects and explore new markets. Mrigendra Bharti Group InfoTech's extensive experience in technology and information services has been a valuable asset, allowing Sellbrochure Vymish Entertainment to integrate advanced digital solutions in its operations, thereby enhancing its distribution capabilities and reader engagement.

Through relentless efforts and a commitment to quality, Sellbrochure Vymish Entertainment continues to break barriers and expand the reach of Indian literature globally. The company's diverse portfolio includes a wide range of genres, catering to different age groups and interests, thereby fostering a rich and inclusive reading culture. As it continues to innovate and grow, Sellbrochure Vymish Entertainment remains dedicated to its mission of making literature accessible to all, contributing significantly to the global literary landscape.

Connect With Mrigendra,
Thank you very much for choosing this book.
You can also connect with me on Instagram,
https://www.instagram.com/i_mrigendrabharti.official
With Love,
Mrigendra Bharti

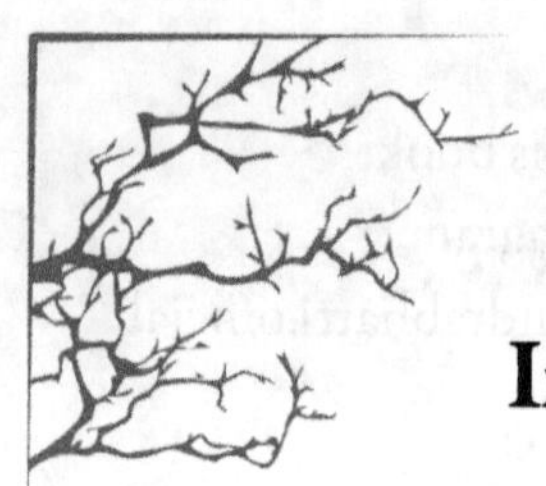

Introduction

In the twilight-drenched realm of Eldoria, whispers slithered through the shadows, chilling tales of a relentless foe – the Shadowbane. This malevolent entity gnawed at the edges of existence, its tendrils of darkness threatening to consume the last vestiges of light. For generations, the people of Eldoria had clung to a fragile hope, their world shrouded in perpetual dusk, a stark contrast to the vibrant dawn they once knew.

This is the story of Seraphina, a young woman ostracized for a darkness that mirrored the encroaching shadows. Unlike others, the darkness within her wasn't a source of fear, but a hidden well of untapped potential. Yet, it was this very darkness that marked her as different, an outcast in a world desperately clinging to light.

As the whispers of the Shadowbane grew louder, an ancient prophecy resurfaced, a chilling portent of a chosen one. This prophesied figure, marked by an affinity for darkness, would either embrace the curse of the Obsidian Heart – a legendary artifact of unimaginable power – or become the instrument of its destruction.

When the whispers morph into a deafening roar, Seraphina finds herself thrust into the heart of this prophecy. The fate of Eldoria rests upon her shoulders, forcing her to confront not only the monstrous entities of Shadowfell, but also the darkness that resides within herself.

This is a tale of courage forged in the face of fear, of understanding blooming amidst ignorance, and of a world on the brink of confronting the delicate balance between light and shadow. Prepare to delve into a realm where darkness whispers secrets and shadows dance with deadly intent. Join Seraphina on a perilous journey into the heart of Shadowfell, where the fate of Eldoria hangs precariously in the balance, and the curse of the Obsidian Heart awaits.

Chapter 1: The Burden of the Curse

The wind howled a mournful tune through the gnarled branches of the nightshade trees, their inky blossoms casting grotesque shadows across the cobblestone path. Seraphina pulled her cloak tighter, the worn fabric offering scant protection from the biting chill that permeated the night. The village of Aethel lay shrouded in darkness, its inhabitants long retired behind bolted doors and shuttered windows. Seraphina, however, was an outsider, forever banished from the warmth and safety it offered.

She quickened her pace, her boots crunching on the frost-dusted stones. The full moon, an ominous orb hanging low in the inky sky, cast an ethereal glow on her face, revealing the heart-shaped locket nestled against her collarbone. Its silver surface gleamed faintly, a stark contrast to the obsidian heart that pulsed beneath it, a constant, heavy reminder of the curse that had ostracized her since birth.

Legends whispered of a time before, when Eldoria thrived under the benevolent rule of the Luminari, their hearts glowing with celestial light. Then came the Shadowbane, a creeping darkness that corrupted the hearts of men, twisting the Luminari's power into a force of destruction. Seraphina, born with an obsidian heart, a mark of the Shadowbane's touch, was deemed a harbinger of doom.

Reaching the village outskirts, Seraphina paused at the base of Aethel's towering stone wall. A single, ornately carved gate stood ajar, a silent invitation for her to leave, an age-old reminder of her place – on the desolate fringes, forever separated from the life she could never have. With a deep, shuddering breath, she stepped through the gate, the groan of rusty hinges echoing in the stillness of the night.

The wind seemed to pick up, swirling around her in a chilling embrace. The nightshade blossoms swayed, their inky petals raining down like whispers of malevolent intent. Seraphina pressed on, her heart hammering a frantic rhythm against her ribs. The weight of loneliness, a constant companion, pressed down upon her, a suffocating cloak heavier than the one she wore.

Tears stung her eyes, blurring the path ahead. She wasn't always this solitary creature. She used to have a family, a life within the village walls. But the whispers started early, fueled by fear and superstition. The day the village healer confirmed the obsidian heart beneath her skin, her world shattered. Her parents, their faces etched with a mixture of grief and terror, were forced to banish her, to protect the village from the alleged darkness she embodied.

A choked sob escaped her lips. Ten years of isolation had etched lines of sorrow on her face, her once vibrant spirit dimmed by the relentless weight of her ostracized existence. Yet, amidst the despair, a flicker of defiance remained. She wouldn't let the curse break her. She would find a way to control it, to prove them all wrong.

The desolate path snaked deeper into the Nightshade Forest, the dense canopy overhead blocking out the moon's faint glow. Seraphina, her senses on high alert, navigated the treacherous terrain with practiced ease. Years of wandering these woods had made them a begrudging haven, a place where she could be alone with her thoughts and the churning darkness within her.

Tonight, however, the familiar solitude felt unsettling. An unnatural stillness hung heavy in the air, broken only by the occasional rustle of unseen creatures in the undergrowth.

Seraphina reached into her cloak, her fingers brushing against the worn hilt of the dagger strapped to her thigh – a small comfort against the unseen dangers that lurked in the shadows.

As she pressed on, a prickling sensation crawled up her spine. It wasn't the usual cold dread that accompanied her solitude; this felt different, a deeper, more primal sense of unease. Glancing around, she strained to pierce the darkness, her heart hammering a frantic tattoo against her ribs.

A twig snapped from somewhere ahead, the sound sharp and sudden in the oppressive silence. Seraphina froze, her hand instinctively tightening around the dagger's hilt. Taking a deep breath, she forced herself forward, her steps measured and silent. The forest floor seemed to absorb every sound, leaving her movements shrouded in an unsettling quiet.

Then, she saw it. A flicker of movement between the gnarled trunks of the trees, a fleeting glimpse of something dark and hulking. Adrenaline surged through her veins, momentarily banishing the cold that had seeped into her bones. Whatever it was, it was large and predatory, and it was watching her.

Panic threatened to consume her, but Seraphina quelled it with a fierce determination. She wouldn't be prey. Not tonight. With a newfound resolve, she crouched low, using the darkness and the thick undergrowth to her advantage. She needed to get closer, to see what she was dealing with.

The creature moved again, this time emerging from behind a massive oak, its form partially obscured by the shadows. Seraphina's breath caught in her throat. It was a monstrosity unlike anything she had ever encountered, a grotesque fusion of wolf and shadow, its eyes glowing with an unnatural red light.

The beast let out a low growl, the sound vibrating through the earth and sending shivers down her spine. It stalked towards her, its movements predatory and deliberate. Seraphina knew she couldn't outrun it. She had to fight.

Gripping her dagger tighter, she stood her ground, her heart pounding a frantic rhythm against her ribs. The creature reared up on its hind legs, its massive form blotting out the moonlight for a fleeting moment. Then, with a bone-chilling roar, it lunged.

Seraphina reacted instinctively, dodging the creature's razor-sharp claws by a hair's breadth. The beast landed with a heavy thud, the ground shaking beneath its immense weight. Adrenaline coursed through her veins, momentarily banishing the fear that threatened to paralyze her. She knew she couldn't fight it with brute strength; she had to be smarter, faster.

Rolling away from another lunging attack, Seraphina scrambled to her feet. Her eyes darted around, searching for an escape route, but the dense undergrowth offered scant refuge. The creature loomed over her, its fetid breath washing over her face. In that moment, a surge of raw emotion welled up within her – a potent cocktail of fear, anger, and a desperate yearning for survival.

And then, something unexpected happened. A tremor ran through her body, starting deep within her core, where the obsidian heart pulsed beneath her skin. The familiar coldness transformed into a searing heat, spreading outwards like wildfire. Instinctively, she reached for the locket around her neck, the silver cool against her burning palm.

A gasp escaped her lips as a wave of energy erupted from the obsidian heart, coursing through her veins with unimaginable power. The world seemed to slow down, the creature's menacing form momentarily frozen in time. Seraphina felt a surge of power unlike anything she had ever known, a primal force that resonated with the darkness within her.

Before the creature could react, Seraphina lashed out. With a newfound strength that belied her slender frame, she raised her dagger, its blade imbued with an otherworldly glow. The air crackled with raw energy as she plunged the dagger forward, aiming for the beast's glowing red eyes.

A deafening screech pierced the night as the blade made contact. The creature recoiled, its massive form twisting in agony. A wave of dark energy surged from the dagger, searing into the beast's flesh and leaving smoldering wounds. The creature roared again, a sound laced with fury and pain, before scrambling back into the darkness of the forest.

Seraphina watched it disappear, her body trembling with the aftereffects of the immense power she had unleashed. The heat had subsided, leaving behind a chilling emptiness. Her heart hammered against her ribs, a frantic drumbeat echoing in the sudden silence.

What had just happened? Had she used the power of the obsidian heart? But how? The questions swirled in her mind, unanswered and unsettling. As the weight of what she had done settled upon her, a new kind of fear gripped her – a fear not of the creature, but of the darkness she now felt thrumming within herself.

Seraphina sank to her knees, the cold dampness of the forest floor seeping through her cloak. Her breaths came in ragged gasps, her body drained from the exertion and the overwhelming power she had wielded. The forest, once a familiar haven, now seemed to echo with a menacing silence, broken only by the frantic beat of her own heart.

Hesitantly, she reached for the locket around her neck, the silver cool against her trembling fingers. The obsidian heart beneath it felt different, a faint thrumming emanating from its depths, a constant reminder of the power she had unleashed. Fear mingled with a strange sense of exhilaration. It was terrifying, this darkness within her, yet undeniably potent.

A twig snapped from somewhere in the distance, sending a fresh jolt of fear through her. But this time, it was different. The fear wasn't paralyzing; it was laced with a newfound awareness, a sense of the power she now possessed. Rising to her feet, she clutched the locket tighter, a silent shield against the unknown.

As she emerged from the dense undergrowth and back onto the desolate path, the full moon peeked through the parting clouds, casting an ethereal glow upon the landscape. Seraphina raised her face towards the moon, its light reflecting in her eyes, now imbued with a newfound intensity.

The prophecy echoed in her mind, a chilling reminder of the darkness she was supposed to unleash. But for the first time, a seed of doubt took root. Was the prophecy set in stone? Or could she defy it? Could she learn to control the darkness within her, not succumb to it?

The weight of this newfound choice settled upon her shoulders, heavy and daunting. The path ahead was shrouded in uncertainty. Yet, as she gazed at the moon, a sliver of hope flickered within her. Perhaps, just perhaps, this curse wasn't a sentence, but a twisted gift – a power waiting to be harnessed. But the question remained – would she be its master, or would it consume her?

With a newfound resolve, Seraphina straightened her shoulders and set off back towards the village outskirts. The path ahead was far from clear, but she wouldn't face it alone. The darkness within her was a burden, but it was also a part of her. And for the first time, she was determined to learn its secrets.

Chapter 2: Unveiling the Past

A cold sweat slicked Seraphina's skin as she jolted awake, the remnants of a nightmare clinging to her like a shroud. The dream, a recurring torment that had plagued her for years, played out in vivid detail. A desolate wasteland, scorched by an unseen fire, stretched as far as the eye could see. In the distance, a towering figure wreathed in shadow loomed, its form radiating an aura of unimaginable power.

Seraphina gasped, her heart pounding a frantic tattoo against her ribs. The figure, faceless yet menacingly familiar, was the embodiment of the ancient evil – the Shadowbane – that according to legend, threatened to consume Eldoria. But the most terrifying aspect of the dream wasn't the Shadowbane itself; it was the undeniable pull she felt towards it, a dark current tugging at the very core of her being.

Throwing back the threadbare covers of her makeshift bed in the abandoned shack that served as her only refuge, Seraphina rose and walked to the lone window. A sliver of dawn light peeked through the cracks in the boarded-up windows, casting an eerie glow on the dusty interior. The weight of the dream pressed down upon her, a suffocating reminder of the darkness she harbored within.

The past ten years of ostracized existence had been a constant struggle. Not just against the villagers' fear and mistrust, but also against the ever-present darkness that thrummed beneath her skin. The memory of the night she'd unleashed the obsidian heart's power in the forest was both exhilarating and terrifying. It was a stark reminder of the raw, untamed power she possessed, a power that both fascinated and repelled her.

But the dream had ignited a new urgency within her. She couldn't simply survive, constantly fearing the darkness within. She needed to understand it, to learn to control it. Perhaps then, she could defy the prophecy and carve her own destiny.

With a newfound resolve, Seraphina straightened her shoulders and began her preparations for the day. The first step, she decided, was to seek knowledge. The village elder, Elara, a wizened woman rumored to possess forgotten lore, was her only hope. But approaching Elara was a risk. The elder had always maintained a neutral stance towards Seraphina, a sliver of compassion amidst the sea of fear. But venturing into the village, even for a brief encounter, could reignite the villagers' anxieties.

Yet, the potential reward – knowledge that could help her control the darkness – outweighed the risk. Taking a deep breath, Seraphina donned her worn cloak, the familiar weight offering a strange sense of comfort. Today, she wouldn't be a pariah seeking solace. Today, she would be a seeker of knowledge, venturing into the heart of the village to confront her past and, perhaps, rewrite her future.

The midday sun beat down mercilessly on Seraphina as she approached the village. The once-familiar cobblestone streets now seemed alien, abuzz with activity and the cheerful chatter of its inhabitants. Glancing around cautiously, she noted the wary glances cast her way. Ten years of isolation had made her a stranger in her own village.

Reaching Elara's cottage, a quaint structure nestled amidst a vibrant flower garden, Seraphina hesitated. The last time she'd crossed Elara's threshold, she was a young girl, ostracized but not yet hardened by years of solitude. Taking a deep breath, she knocked on the weathered oak door.

A long moment passed before the door creaked open, revealing Elara's wizened face. Her eyes, usually filled with a quiet wisdom, widened in surprise at the sight of Seraphina. A flicker of something akin to pity crossed her features, quickly replaced by a stoic mask.

"Seraphina," Elara acknowledged, her voice raspy with age. "This is a surprise."

"Elara," Seraphina replied, her voice hoarse with disuse. "I need your help."

Elara studied her for a long moment, her silence heavy with unspoken emotions. Finally, she sighed and stepped aside, allowing Seraphina to enter. The small cottage, filled with the scent of dried herbs and old books, felt like a haven from the harsh judgment of the outside world.

Seraphina found herself seated at a worn table, a steaming cup of herbal tea cradled in her hands. The warmth seeped through her chilled fingers, offering a small comfort. Elara remained silent, her gaze fixed on the flickering flames in the hearth.

"I know why you're here, child," Elara finally spoke, her voice low and filled with a hint of sadness. "The nightmares plague you again."

Seraphina nodded, the memory of the dream still vivid in her mind. "They're getting worse, Elara. I... I don't understand."

Elara rose from her chair and walked over to a weathered bookshelf, her gnarled fingers trailing across the aged spines. After a moment, she pulled out a thick, leather-bound tome, its surface etched with strange symbols. Returning to the table, she placed the book before Seraphina.

"This is the Chronicle of Luminari," Elara explained. "It contains the forgotten history of Eldoria, a time before the Shadowbane's corruption."

Seraphina traced the symbols on the book's cover, a strange sense of anticipation tingling down her spine. "Do you think it can help me?" she whispered, her voice barely above a breath.

Elara met her gaze, a flicker of hope battling with trepidation in her eyes. "Knowledge is a weapon, Seraphina. But it can also be a burden. Are you prepared to wield it?"

Seraphina stared at the ancient tome, the weight of Elara's words settling upon her. Knowledge was a double-edged sword, she understood. It could offer the answers she craved, the key to controlling the darkness within. But it could also unveil truths too terrible to bear, secrets that could shatter the fragile hope she clung to.

Taking a deep breath, she met Elara's gaze. Fear flickered in her eyes, but it was overshadowed by a steely determination. "I am," she rasped, her voice firm. "I have to be."

Elara nodded, a hint of approval flickering in her aged eyes. With trembling fingers, she opened the Chronicle of Luminari, revealing pages filled with faded script and intricate illustrations. The air crackled with an unseen energy as Elara began to speak, her voice weaving a tale lost to the ages.

She spoke of the Luminari, their hearts glowing with celestial light, guardians of Eldoria who protected the realm from the encroaching darkness. Then came the Shadowbane, a creeping evil that twisted the hearts of men, corrupting the Luminari's power. The war that ensued was long and brutal, leaving Eldoria forever scarred.

Seraphina listened intently, her heart pounding against her ribs. Elara's words painted a vivid picture of a glorious past and a terrifying present. But as Elara delved deeper into the history of the obsidian hearts, a coldness spread through Seraphina.

The ancient texts spoke of the Luminari's failed attempts to purge the darkness, to cleanse the hearts tainted by the Shadowbane. The obsidian heart, they claimed, was a mark of ultimate corruption, a harbinger of doom. Despair threatened to consume Seraphina. Was she truly destined to become the embodiment of evil, a pawn in the Shadowbane's game?

Elara sensed her growing despair and placed a wrinkled hand over hers. "The chronicles are but one perspective, child," she said gently. "There are whispers of a different kind of obsidian heart, one that held the potential to not only resist the darkness but to extinguish it altogether."

A spark of hope ignited within Seraphina. Could this be true? Was there a possibility that the prophecy was not set in stone? Elara squeezed her hand, her eyes filled with a newfound determination.

"There is much we don't know, Seraphina," Elara continued. "But together, we will delve deeper. We will find the truth about your heart and the power it holds."

A sliver of hope, fragile yet tenacious, bloomed in Seraphina's chest. The possibility of the obsidian heart being a force for good, a weapon against the darkness, was a revelation that challenged everything she thought she knew. Elara's unwavering support, a beacon of kindness in a world of fear, fueled Seraphina's resolve.

"Where do we begin?" Seraphina asked, her voice trembling with a mix of hope and trepidation.

Elara's brow furrowed as she surveyed the room. Her gaze landed on a dusty tapestry hanging on the far wall, depicting a map of Eldoria etched with faded markings. "There are legends," she began, her voice raspy, "of a hidden library, a repository of forgotten knowledge said to be guarded by the Order of the Arcane."

Seraphina's breath hitched. The Order of the Arcane, a brotherhood of mages skilled in wielding ancient magic, was shrouded in mystery. They were rumored to have vanished centuries ago, their secrets lost to time.

"But the Order is just a myth," Seraphina stammered, voicing the doubt that gnawed at her.

Elara shook her head. "Perhaps. But the library, if it exists, could hold the answers you seek. However, reaching it won't be easy. The path is fraught with danger, and the guardians, if they still exist, may not be welcoming."

A knot of apprehension tightened in Seraphina's stomach. Venturing beyond the village was risky, venturing into the rumored location of the Arcane library felt like a fool's errand. Yet, the potential reward – knowledge to control the darkness and defy the prophecy – outweighed the fear.

"I'll go," Seraphina declared, her voice firm despite the tremor in her heart. "I have to try."

Elara studied her with a mix of concern and admiration. "This path you choose, Seraphina, is not for the faint of heart. It will test your strength, your courage, and perhaps even your sanity. Are you certain you're prepared?"

Seraphina met Elara's gaze, her eyes blazing with newfound determination. "The nightmares won't stop, Elara," she said, her voice ringing with conviction. "The darkness within me grows stronger with each passing day. I have to find a way to control it, or it will consume me. This is my only chance."

Elara placed a hand on Seraphina's shoulder, her touch surprisingly strong. "Then let us begin," she said, a glint of determination in her eyes. "The road ahead will be perilous, but you won't face it alone."

A silent pact was forged in that moment, a bond between an ostracized girl and a wise elder, united against a darkness that threatened to consume them all. As Elara unveiled a hidden compartment within the bookshelf, revealing a collection of ancient scrolls and cryptic maps, Seraphina knew her life was about to change forever. The journey to the Arcane library, fraught with danger and uncertainty, was just the beginning. The true test would lie in unlocking the secrets of the obsidian heart and wielding its power – a power that could be her salvation or her doom.

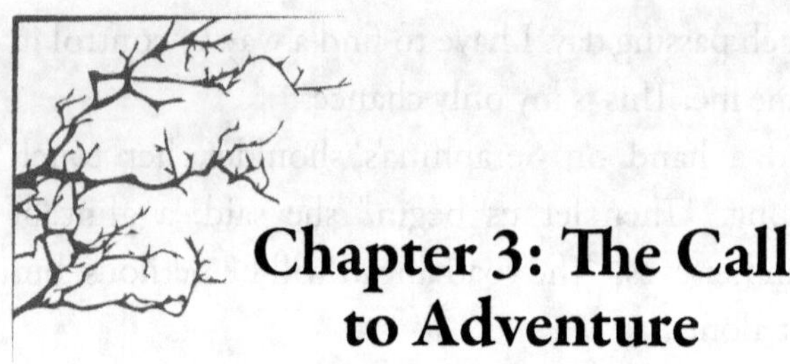

Chapter 3: The Call
to Adventure

Days bled into weeks as Seraphina and Elara pored over the cryptic scrolls and maps unearthed from the hidden compartment. Deciphering the faded script and arcane symbols presented a daunting challenge, but Seraphina's determination burned bright. Each night, fueled by Elara's sage guidance, they chipped away at the mysteries, piecing together clues about the fabled Arcane library.

The journey, they discovered, would be arduous. The library's location remained shrouded in legend, rumored to lie deep within the Whispering Woods, a sprawling expanse of ancient oaks and tangled undergrowth. Legends whispered of the woods being a haven for fantastical creatures and malevolent spirits, a place where the very air crackled with a sense of foreboding.

Despite the growing unease in her gut, Seraphina pushed forward. The nightmares, once sporadic, became nightly visitors, leaving her drained and desperate. The darkness within her, a constant thrumming beneath her skin, seemed to grow bolder with each passing day. Learning to control it, the scrolls hinted, was the key to unlocking the true potential of the obsidian heart.

One crisp autumn morning, as the first blush of dawn painted the sky, Seraphina stood on the outskirts of the village, Elara by her side. A knapsack, filled with provisions and Elara's carefully chosen potions, hung heavy on Seraphina's back. The weight of it paled in comparison to the burden she carried within – the obsidian heart and the weight of the unknown.

Elara gripped Seraphina's hand, her wrinkled face etched with a mix of concern and pride. "The path ahead is treacherous, child," she said, her voice raspy. "Remember, the darkness within can be your ally or your enemy. Learn to control it, and it will become your greatest strength."

Seraphina took a deep breath, the crisp morning air filling her lungs. "I will," she promised, her voice unwavering. "I won't let the darkness consume me."

Elara nodded, her eyes filled with a flicker of hope. Then, with a farewell gesture, she turned and retreated back into the familiar embrace of the village. Seraphina watched her go, a knot of apprehension tightening in her stomach. She was alone now, venturing into the unknown, a solitary figure on the cusp of an adventure that would change her destiny.

Taking another deep breath, Seraphina cast one last glance back at the village walls, the remnants of her past life. With a newfound resolve, she turned and stepped into the Whispering Woods. The canopy of ancient oaks closed over her, casting the forest floor in perpetual twilight. The air hung heavy with the scent of damp earth and decaying leaves, and an unsettling silence pressed in on her, broken only by the rustle of unseen creatures.

As Seraphina ventured deeper, a prickling sensation crawled up her spine. It wasn't the familiar fear, but something different, a primal awareness. The darkness within her, usually a dull thrumming, pulsed with a newfound energy, resonating with the whispers that seemed to emanate from the surrounding trees. Taking a deep breath, Seraphina tightened her grip on the hilt of the dagger strapped to her thigh. The journey had begun, and she wasn't sure what awaited her in the depths of the Whispering Woods, but one thing was certain – she wouldn't be alone. The darkness within her was awake, and for the first time, she was ready to listen.

The whispers started subtly, a mere rustling of leaves or the sigh of the wind through the gnarled branches. But as Seraphina ventured deeper into the Whispering Woods, they grew clearer, taking on a seductive, almost hypnotic quality. They spoke in an unknown tongue, filled with promises of power and forgotten knowledge.

Seraphina pressed on, her steps cautious and measured. The path, barely discernible beneath a thick blanket of fallen leaves, seemed to twist and turn on its own, leading her deeper into the heart of the ancient forest. The whispers grew bolder, weaving tales of forgotten civilizations and lost magic, offering glimpses of the power the Arcane library held.

But with each alluring whisper, a tremor of unease ran through Seraphina. The darkness within her thrummed in response, its power resonating with the voices in the wind. It urged her to succumb, to embrace the power they offered, promising to fulfill her every desire.

Suddenly, a flash of movement caught her eye. A shadowy figure darted between the trees, its form shrouded in the twilight. Fear, cold and primal, gripped Seraphina. Was it a creature lured by the whispers? Or something more sinister, drawn to the darkness thrumming within her?

Gripping her dagger tighter, Seraphina strained to see through the dense foliage. The figure reappeared, closer this time, its eyes glowing with an unnatural red light. A low growl rumbled through the woods, sending shivers down her spine. The whispers, once seductive, now carried a tinge of malice, urging her to unleash the growing power within.

But Seraphina held firm. The image of Elara's concerned face flashed in her mind, her words echoing in the silence: "The darkness can be your enemy or your ally." Taking a deep breath, she focused on the memory of the Chronicle of Luminari. The Luminari, with their hearts of pure light, had fought against the darkness. She could do the same.

With newfound resolve, she channeled the growing power within, not to unleash it, but to push back against the whispers. A surge of energy erupted from her core, a wave of resistance that echoed through the woods. The whispers faltered, then retreated, leaving behind an unsettling silence.

The shadowy figure hesitated, its glowing eyes fixed on Seraphina. Then, with a final menacing growl, it melted back into the undergrowth, vanishing into the twilight. Seraphina stood her ground, her heart pounding against her ribs. The encounter had been a stark reminder of the dangers lurking within the Whispering Woods, but also of her own strength.

She had faced the darkness within and emerged victorious. It was a small victory, but it gave her hope. The journey ahead would be fraught with peril, but she wouldn't face it alone. She had Elara's teachings to guide her, the whispers as a cautionary tale, and the growing potential of the obsidian heart simmering within her.

Taking another deep breath, Seraphina continued her trek, the whispers now replaced by a determined silence. The path ahead remained shrouded in mystery, but she was no longer just a scared outcast. Now, she was a seeker of knowledge, a warrior against the darkness, and most importantly, she was the bearer of the obsidian heart – a potential force for good waiting to be unleashed. The journey to the Arcane library had just begun, and Seraphina was ready to embrace the adventure, whatever challenges it may hold.

Days bled into one another as Seraphina navigated the seemingly endless maze of the Whispering Woods. The canopy of ancient oaks blocked out most of the sunlight, leaving the forest floor in a perpetual twilight. The only sounds were the rustle of unseen creatures and the relentless whisper of the wind through the leaves.

Hunger gnawed at her stomach, and exhaustion weighed heavily on her limbs. But the thought of turning back, of succumbing to her doubts, never crossed her mind. The memory of her recurring nightmare, the image of the Shadowbane looming large, fueled her determination. She had to find a way to control the darkness, or it would eventually consume her.

One evening, as the last rays of the setting sun cast long shadows through the trees, Seraphina stumbled upon a clearing. In the center stood a single, magnificent oak, its branches reaching towards the sky like gnarled fingers. An unsettling aura emanated from it, a sense of ancient power that sent shivers down her spine.

As she approached the oak, the whispers that had been a constant presence since entering the woods intensified. They spoke in the same unknown tongue, but this time, they carried a different tone – a sense of urgency, almost desperation.

Hesitantly, Seraphina touched the rough bark of the oak. A surge of energy crackled through her, a connection so profound it left her breathless. It was as if the tree itself was alive, pulsating with an ancient magic that resonated with the obsidian heart beneath her skin.

Suddenly, the clearing shifted around her. The ancient oak blurred, the ground beneath her feet turned to swirling mist. Disoriented and afraid, Seraphina stumbled back, a gasp escaping her lips. Her world dissolved into a chaotic mix of colors and sounds, then darkness.

When she regained consciousness, she found herself lying on a cold stone floor. The air was thick with the musty scent of old books and forgotten lore. Groaning, she sat up, taking in her surroundings.

She was in a vast chamber, its walls lined with towering shelves overflowing with ancient tomes. An ethereal glow emanated from the books, casting strange shadows across the room. In the center stood a lone figure, cloaked in a dark robe, its face obscured by a hood.

The figure turned towards Seraphina, its eyes burning with an unnatural light. A low rumble echoed through the chamber, a voice that seemed to emanate from the very walls themselves. "Welcome, child of the obsidian heart," it boomed. "You have come seeking knowledge."

Seraphina's heart pounded against her ribs. Who was this mysterious figure? Guardian or trickster? Ally or enemy? Taking a deep breath, she forced her voice to remain steady. "I am," she replied, rising to her feet. "I seek knowledge to control the darkness within me."

The figure tilted its head, studying her with an intensity that made Seraphina squirm under its gaze. "The darkness can be a powerful tool," it rumbled. "But it can also be your undoing."

A shiver ran down Seraphina's spine. These were the same warnings Elara had given her. Was this a test? A chance to prove her intentions?

"I know the risks," she said, her voice firm. "But I choose to fight the darkness, not surrender to it. I need the knowledge to do so."

The figure remained silent for a long moment, the tension in the chamber thick enough to cut with a knife. Finally, it spoke, its voice softer this time. "Very well, child of the obsidian heart. The knowledge you seek can be found within these walls. But be warned, the path to understanding is fraught with danger. Are you prepared to face it?"

Seraphina didn't hesitate. She had come too far to turn back now. "I am," she declared, her voice ringing with newfound determination. A spark of amusement flickered in the figure's eyes, a flicker that vanished as quickly as it appeared.

"Then let your journey begin," it rumbled. The figure raised a gloved hand, and the shelves lining the chamber swirled, rearranging themselves with a mechanical whir. "Seek the answers you seek, child of the obsidian heart. But remember, knowledge is power, and power comes at a price."

With a final, ominous note hanging in the air, the figure stepped back into the shadows, leaving Seraphina alone amidst the labyrinth of ancient tomes. The true test had only just begun.

The library pulsed with a strange energy, an almost sentient power that hummed beneath Seraphina's skin. The shelves, now reorganized in an intricate pattern, seemed to beckon her forward, promising secrets waiting to be unearthed. But the figure's cryptic words echoed in her mind – "knowledge is power, and power comes at a price."

Taking a deep breath, Seraphina stepped forward. The weight of the unknown pressed down on her, but she was no longer the scared girl fleeing her past. Her gaze scanned the seemingly endless rows of books, searching for a clue, a starting point.

Suddenly, a book on the nearest shelf pulsed with a faint golden light. Drawn by its radiance, Seraphina reached out and carefully pulled it from the shelf. It was bound in worn leather, its cover adorned with intricate symbols that seemed to shimmer under her touch. As she opened it, a wave of energy washed over her, and faded script materialized on the pages.

The book spoke of the ancient history of the obsidian hearts, not as harbingers of doom, but as vessels of immense power. It detailed how the Luminari, with their hearts filled with celestial light, used them to channel their magic, to protect Eldoria from the encroaching darkness.

A spark of hope ignited within Seraphina. Could this be true? Was the prophecy just a misunderstanding? As she delved deeper into the text, her heart sank. The process of harnessing the obsidian heart's power was complex and dangerous. It required a perfect balance of light and shadow within the user's soul – a balance Seraphina was far from achieving.

Disappointment gnawed at her. Had she journeyed so far for nothing? But then, her eyes fell upon a passage detailing a specific meditation technique practiced by the Luminari. It spoke of venturing within oneself, confronting the darkness, and forging a bond with it, not suppressing it.

This resonated with Seraphina. Perhaps the key wasn't in extinguishing the darkness within, but in understanding and controlling it. With newfound determination, she decided to try the meditation technique.

Sitting cross-legged on the cold stone floor, she closed her eyes and focused on her breathing. Images of the nightmare, the Shadowbane looming large, flooded her mind. Fear threatened to engulf her, but she pushed forward, delving deeper.

Then, she felt it – a presence within her, a swirling vortex of darkness and power. It pulsed in response to her fear, urging her to succumb. But instead of giving in, Seraphina channeled the memory of Elara's teachings, the image of the Luminari channeling their light.

With a surge of willpower, she projected a sliver of light from within, a single spark amidst the encroaching darkness. The darkness recoiled, surprised by the resistance. Then, a flicker of something unexpected – understanding.

The darkness wasn't just a destructive force; it was a part of her, a source of immense power waiting to be harnessed. Slowly, cautiously, Seraphina extended the sliver of light, offering it to the darkness. The encounter wasn't a battle, but a delicate negotiation.

The darkness hesitated, then a tendril of its essence reached out, connecting with the light. It wasn't a complete fusion, but a tentative accord, a symbiotic relationship. A feeling of peace, albeit a tenuous one, settled over Seraphina.

She opened her eyes, the library appearing brighter, the ancient tomes seeming to hold less menace and more promise. The process was far from over, but she had taken the first step. She wasn't just the bearer of the obsidian heart; she was learning to be its master.

As she continued to delve into the library's secrets, Seraphina knew the path ahead would be fraught with danger. But with newfound knowledge and a burgeoning control over the darkness, she faced the future with a newfound confidence. The whispers, now a distant echo, had become a constant reminder – the darkness could be a powerful ally, but it was up to her to choose how to wield it. The journey to the Arcane library had reshaped her, not just with knowledge, but with the power to control her own destiny. And as she ventured deeper into the labyrinth of books, she knew her true adventure was just beginning.

Chapter 4: Whispers of War

Weeks bled into months as Seraphina delved deeper into the secrets of the Arcane library. The once-daunting labyrinth of books became a familiar haven, its ancient tomes whispering forgotten lore into her eager ears. The knowledge she gleaned was a potent mix – intricate rituals practiced by the Luminari, cryptic warnings about the encroaching Shadowbane, and most importantly, the true potential of the obsidian heart.

The process of mastering the obsidian heart remained a constant challenge. Every night, she ventured within, facing the swirling vortex of darkness that resided within her. But each encounter chipped away at the fear, replacing it with a growing understanding. She learned to navigate the darkness, not as a destroyer, but as a collaborator. It craved power, and she offered it a controlled release, channeling its chaotic energy into focused bursts of strength and agility.

With each passing day, Seraphina grew stronger, both physically and mentally. The nightmares, once a nightly torment, became less frequent, replaced by vivid dreams of the Luminari, their celestial hearts glowing with an otherworldly light. The dreams offered a glimpse of what she could become, a beacon of hope in a world shrouded in darkness.

One crisp morning, as Seraphina emerged from a particularly enlightening meditation session, the air shimmered with an unsettling energy. The whispers, long subdued, returned, this time carrying a sense of urgency and fear. They spoke of a dark force rising, of the Shadowbane's grip tightening around Eldoria.

Terror gripped Seraphina's heart. Had her journey taken too long? Had the Shadowbane already made its move? Her newfound confidence faltered, replaced by a cold dread. But then, a wave of defiant resolve washed over her. She wouldn't let fear cripple her. The knowledge she had gained, the power she wielded – it was all meant for this moment.

Following the whispers, she navigated deeper into the library, her steps quickened by a newfound urgency. She stumbled upon a hidden chamber, its entrance obscured by a tapestry depicting a map of Eldoria, dark tendrils emanating from a central point. In the center of the map pulsed a crimson mark, sending shivers down Seraphina's spine.

The whispers intensified, forming a single chilling word: "Shadowfell." It resonated within her, a location of immense power, the potential birthplace of the Shadowbane's resurgence. It was there, deep within the corrupted heart of Eldoria, that the final battle would be fought.

Dread and hope warred within Seraphina. The revelation was terrifying - the Shadowbane was closer than she imagined. But it was also a beacon. By confronting the source of the darkness, she could potentially stop its spread and fulfill her destiny as the true wielder of the obsidian heart.

As she stood there, the weight of responsibility settling on her shoulders, a lone figure emerged from the shadows of the chamber. The cloaked figure, the guardian of the library, materialized before her, its eyes glowing with an eerie light.

"You have learned much, child of the obsidian heart," the figure rumbled, its voice echoing through the chamber. "The time has come for you to leave this haven and face your destiny."

Seraphina took a deep breath, her gaze unwavering. "I know," she replied, her voice ringing with newfound conviction. "Where can I find Shadowfell?"

The figure raised a gloved hand, and the map on the tapestry shimmered. The crimson mark pulsed with an intense light, then a path, a network of glowing lines, appeared across the map, leading directly to Shadowfell.

"This path will guide you," the figure intoned. "But remember, the journey will be perilous. The fate of Eldoria rests upon your shoulders, child of the obsidian heart. Will you answer the call?"

Seraphina straightened her shoulders, the resolve burning bright within her. "I will," she declared, her voice echoing through the chamber. The weight of the past, the burden of her destiny, all seemed lighter now. She was no longer just a girl ostracized by her village. She was Seraphina, bearer of the obsidian heart, and the last hope for a world teetering on the brink of darkness. With a newfound purpose coursing through her veins, Seraphina stepped out of the Arcane library, ready to answer the call and face whatever challenges awaited her on the path to Shadowfell. The whispers, once a source of fear, now served as a guiding voice, a reminder of the darkness she had to confront, and the power she wielded to overcome it.

Leaving the comforting embrace of the Arcane library behind, Seraphina emerged into the familiar gloom of the Whispering Woods. The whispers, once subdued, now echoed with renewed urgency, guiding her towards the path revealed on the map. It was a treacherous route, marked by jagged mountain ranges and desolate wastelands, a stark contrast to the dense canopy she had grown accustomed to.

The weight of the revelation settled upon her shoulders. Shadowfell, the birthplace of the encroaching darkness, loomed large in her mind. The knowledge was empowering, but also terrifying. Confronting the source of the corruption felt like a suicide mission, yet the alternative – succumbing to the Shadowbane's growing power – was unthinkable.

As she ventured deeper into the wilderness, the whispers intensified, painting a chilling picture of Shadowfell. They spoke of a desolate landscape shrouded in perpetual twilight, a place where twisted creatures roamed freely, corrupted by the Shadowbane's influence.

Seraphina pressed on, fueled by a mix of fear and determination. The days bled into weeks, marked by relentless treks and encounters with fantastical creatures, their forms warped by the encroaching darkness. Yet, with each challenge overcome, Seraphina grew stronger, her control over the obsidian heart solidifying with each passing moment.

One evening, as she huddled around a crackling fire, a sense of foreboding settled over her. The whispers, usually a steady hum in the back of her mind, morphed into a frantic screech, warning of a danger lurking ahead. Gripping the hilt of her dagger, she rose to her feet, her senses on high alert.

Suddenly, a horde of nightmarish creatures emerged from the shadows. Their bodies, grotesque parodies of familiar animals, were twisted by the Shadowbane's corruption. Their glowing red eyes burned with a malevolent hunger, and their guttural growls echoed through the night.

Seraphina knew there was no time for fear. With a surge of adrenaline, she channeled the obsidian heart's power. A wave of energy erupted from her core, a shimmering shield that repelled the initial charge of the creatures. But there were too many, their relentless assault pushing her back.

Just as despair threatened to engulf her, a memory surfaced in her mind – a passage from a dusty tome in the Arcane library. It spoke of a defensive maneuver utilized by the Luminari, a way to channel the obsidian heart's power to create a protective barrier.

Focusing her will, Seraphina visualized the technique. The energy radiating from her core intensified, coalescing into a shimmering dome that enveloped her. The creatures slammed against the barrier, their claws raking ineffectively against the shimmering energy.

Emboldened by this success, Seraphina didn't just defend. With a surge of controlled fury, she channeled the obsidian heart's offensive potential. Blasts of dark energy erupted from her fingertips, striking down the creatures with deadly accuracy. The air crackled with power, and the stench of burnt flesh filled the air.

The battle raged on through the night, but slowly, the tide began to turn. The creatures, weakened by Seraphina's relentless assault, began to falter. One by one, they fell, their lifeless bodies littering the forest floor.

As dawn broke, painting the sky with streaks of orange and pink, the last creature retreated back into the shadows. Seraphina stood amidst the carnage, her body trembling with exhaustion, but a fierce resolve burning in her eyes. She had faced the darkness head-on and emerged victorious.

This encounter served as a stark reminder of the challenges that awaited her on the path to Shadowfell. Yet, it also instilled a newfound confidence in her abilities. She was no longer just a girl with a cursed heart; she was a warrior, a beacon of hope against the encroaching darkness.

With a deep breath, Seraphina extinguished the dying embers of her fire and shouldered her pack. The journey ahead was far from over, but she was ready. The whispers, once a source of fear, now served as a battle cry, urging her forward towards Shadowfell. The fate of Eldoria rested on her shoulders, and she wouldn't falter. She would confront the darkness at its source and emerge victorious, or die trying.

The landscape grew harsher as Seraphina ventured deeper into the uncharted territory leading to Shadowfell. Lush forests gave way to barren plains, the once vibrant sky replaced by a perpetual twilight that cast long, menacing shadows. The whispers grew stronger, a chilling symphony of despair and dread that gnawed at Seraphina's spirit. Gone were the warnings of specific dangers; now they spoke of a suffocating darkness, an all-encompassing void that promised oblivion.

Days blurred into one another, marked by a relentless journey across the desolate expanse. The obsidian heart thrummed within her chest, a constant reminder of the power and the burden she carried. Hunger gnawed at her stomach, and exhaustion weighed heavily on her limbs, but she dared not falter. Each step brought her closer to Shadowfell, closer to confronting the source of the encroaching darkness.

One evening, as Seraphina camped amidst the ruins of a long-forgotten civilization, a flicker of movement caught her eye. A lone figure, cloaked in a tattered black robe, materialized from the shadows. It moved with an unnatural grace, its face hidden beneath a hood, but Seraphina felt a prickle of unease crawl up her spine.

The figure stopped a few paces from her fire, its presence sending a shiver down her spine. "You are far from home, child of the obsidian heart," a raspy voice emanated from beneath the hood.

Seraphina gripped the hilt of her dagger, her gaze wary. "Who are you?" she demanded, her voice hoarse from disuse.

The figure chuckled, a dry, humorless sound. "A traveler," it replied. "One who has witnessed the rise of the Shadowbane and the fall of countless heroes who dared to oppose it."

A wave of unease washed over Seraphina. This wasn't a mere passerby. This figure exuded an aura of power, a power tinged with something akin to despair.

"Why are you here?" she pressed, her voice unwavering despite the tremor in her heart.

A long silence followed. Then, the figure spoke again, its voice low and melancholic. "To warn you, child. Turn back. The darkness of Shadowfell is not something you can hope to overcome."

Seraphina's resolve hardened. This was a ploy, an attempt to sow doubt and fear. "I will not turn back," she declared, her voice ringing with defiance. "The fate of Eldoria rests on my shoulders."

The figure let out another dry chuckle. "A noble sentiment, child. But one ultimately doomed to fail. The Shadowbane is not a force to be reckoned with. It consumes all who come before it."

Seraphina rose to her feet, her gaze locked on the cloaked figure. "Perhaps," she said, her voice firm. "But I won't go down without a fight."

The figure tilted its head, studying her with an intensity that made Seraphina squirm under its gaze. "Very well," it finally conceded. "You have a warrior's spirit. But remember, child, even the bravest warrior falls before the overwhelming darkness." With a final, ominous note hanging in the air, the figure turned and melted back into the shadows, leaving Seraphina alone amidst the ruins.

The encounter had shaken her, planting a seed of doubt in her mind. Could the figure be right? Was she marching towards her own destruction? But then, she looked down at her hand, calloused but determined. The memory of the villagers, their terrified faces, fueled her resolve. She couldn't turn back. She had to protect Eldoria, even if it meant sacrificing herself.

Taking a deep breath, Seraphina extinguished the fire. Dawn was still hours away, but she couldn't wait. With renewed determination, she shouldered her pack and set off, driven forward by a single, unshakeable purpose: to reach Shadowfell, confront the source of the darkness, and for the sake of Eldoria, emerge victorious or die trying. The path ahead was shrouded in darkness, filled with the whispers of despair, but Seraphina, the bearer of the obsidian heart, would not falter.

Days bled into weeks as Seraphina trudged through the desolate wasteland. The whispers in her head had morphed from a chilling symphony to a relentless drone, a constant reminder of the oppressive darkness that enveloped Shadowfell. The sun, a once-familiar orb, became a faint, distant memory, replaced by an endless twilight that cast long, skeletal shadows across the barren landscape.

Exhaustion gnawed at her from within, her once vibrant spirit dulled by the ceaseless struggle. Yet, a flicker of defiance remained, fueled by the image of Elara's face, her unwavering belief in the potential of the obsidian heart. It was this memory that propelled Seraphina forward, pushing her to continue when every fiber of her being yearned for rest.

One evening, as she huddled against a jagged rock formation, seeking a fleeting respite from the biting wind, a change in the whispers caught her attention. They no longer spoke of despair, but of a malevolent presence – a throbbing heart of darkness radiating a chilling power. Seraphina recognized it instantly – the heart of the Shadowbane, the source of the encroaching corruption.

A surge of adrenaline coursed through her, a stark contrast to the bone-deep weariness that had settled within. She was close, closer than she had ever imagined. Fear threatened to engulf her, but she pushed it down, channeling it into resolve.

Taking a deep breath, Seraphina rose to her feet. The whispers, now a clear beacon, guided her towards a distant mountain range, jagged peaks piercing the dusky sky. It was there, nestled amidst the treacherous terrain, that the heart of the Shadowbane resided.

The journey towards the mountains was treacherous, a labyrinth of treacherous slopes and treacherous ravines. Every step was a battle against exhaustion, the harsh elements, and the ever-present dread that gnawed at her spirit. Yet, with each obstacle overcome, Seraphina grew stronger, her connection to the obsidian heart solidifying. It thrummed within her chest, a dark counterpoint to the growing malevolent presence that pulsed before her.

Finally, after days of relentless struggle, Seraphina reached the foot of the mountain range. The air grew thick and oppressive, the whispers morphing into a cacophony of torment, urging her to turn back. Ignoring the chilling chorus, Seraphina began her ascent, her resolve hardening with each arduous step.

The climb was a blur of treacherous boulders and icy scree. Yet, Seraphina persevered, her willpower fueled by the knowledge that the fate of Eldoria rested on her shoulders. As she neared the summit, the whispers intensified, laced with a chilling amusement as if the Shadowbane itself felt her approach.

Finally, after what seemed like an eternity, Seraphina emerged onto a desolate plateau. Before her, a monolithic structure of obsidian rose from the barren ground, its dark, polished surface reflecting the faint twilight sky. An aura of pure evil pulsated from the structure, draining the very light from the surroundings.

This was the heart of Shadowfell, the source of the encroaching darkness. Seraphina stood at the precipice of her destiny, her heart hammering against her ribs. The whispers, now a triumphant roar, threatened to drown out the final embers of hope within her.

But then, as she gazed upon the obsidian monolith, a strange feeling washed over her. It wasn't fear, but a deep understanding. The darkness within her, long suppressed, felt a kinship with the heart of Shadowfell. In that moment, Seraphina realized the true challenge lay not just in defeating the Shadowbane, but in controlling the darkness within herself.

Taking a deep breath, Seraphina steeled herself for the battle ahead. This wasn't just a fight against an external enemy, but a confrontation with the darkness that resided within. With newfound resolve, she marched towards the obsidian monolith, the whispers swirling around her like a malevolent storm. The fate of Eldoria hung in the balance, and Seraphina, the bearer of the obsidian heart, was ready to face the darkness head-on.

Chapter 5: Into the Heart of Darkness

The obsidian monolith loomed before Seraphina, its polished surface reflecting the faint twilight in a distorted, nightmarish mirror image. Whispers, now a cacophony of torment and amusement, filled the air, a chilling chorus that threatened to unravel her resolve. Yet, Seraphina stood firm, a warrior poised for battle.

The journey to Shadowfell had tested her in ways she never imagined. The harsh landscapes, the relentless exhaustion, and the constant struggle against the oppressive darkness had chipped away at her physical and mental strength. But within this crucible, a new Seraphina had emerged – hardened, determined, and most importantly, in control of the obsidian heart that pulsed within her chest.

Taking a deep breath, Seraphina closed her eyes, focusing on the familiar thrumming within. It wasn't just a source of power, but a reflection of her own darkness – a darkness she had learned to channel, not suppress. She envisioned the obsidian heart, not as a harbinger of doom, but as a potential tool for good, a force waiting to be unleashed against the true enemy – the Shadowbane.

As she opened her eyes, a wave of confidence washed over her. The whispers, once a source of fear, now served as a battle cry. With a newfound purpose, she strode towards the monolith, the faint twilight shimmering off the polished black surface.

The entrance to the heart of Shadowfell was a gaping maw, a swirling vortex of darkness that pulsed with an unnatural energy. A cold tendril of fear slithered down Seraphina's spine, but she pushed it down. This was it. The moment she had been dreading, yet secretly yearning for.

With a resolute nod, Seraphina stepped into the vortex. The world dissolved into a swirling chaos of darkness and distorted light. Sounds became warped and unrecognizable, replaced by a low, pulsating hum that resonated deep within her bones.

The descent seemed like an eternity, a journey through the very essence of darkness. When Seraphina finally stumbled out of the vortex, she found herself in a cavern unlike any she had ever seen. The walls were slick obsidian, reflecting an eerie red glow emanating from a central structure – a colossal obsidian heart, pulsing with a malevolent power.

Around the heart, shadowy figures writhed, their forms twisted and grotesque, fueled by the darkness radiating from the monolithic heart. They were the Shadowbane's minions, creatures of pure darkness given form.

Seraphina's grip tightened around the hilt of her dagger, a surge of determination coursing through her veins. These were foot soldiers, pawns in a larger game. Her true adversary awaited – the entity behind the Shadowbane, the source of the encroaching darkness itself.

As if sensing her presence, the monolithic heart pulsed with renewed vigor, bathing the cavern in an even more intense red light. The whispers, now a deafening roar, filled the air, assaulting her with visions of pain, despair, and destruction.

But Seraphina held firm. Channeling the obsidian heart within her, she projected a shimmering blade of pure darkness. It pulsed with a different kind of darkness – a controlled, focused darkness fueled by her will.

With a battle cry that echoed through the cavern, Seraphina charged towards the shadowy figures, the flickering blade carving a path through their ranks. The fight was brutal, a whirlwind of claws, fangs, and desperate fury. Yet, with each blow, Seraphina grew stronger, her control over the obsidian heart solidifying.

As the last of the minions fell, the cavern fell silent, save for the pulsating hum of the monolithic heart. Seraphina stood panting amidst the carnage, her body bruised but unbroken. Now, only the entity at the heart of the Shadowbane remained.

Taking a deep breath, Seraphina steeled her nerves and began her ascent towards the monolithic heart. As she drew closer, the whispers intensified, urging her to succumb, to become part of the darkness. But Seraphina ignored them, her gaze fixed on the entity residing within the heart.

And there, bathed in the crimson glow, she saw it – not a monstrous creature, but a swirling vortex of pure darkness, a primal force devoid of form or reason. It was the embodiment of all negativity, the absence of light, the source of the encroaching darkness that threatened to consume Eldoria.

For a moment, Seraphina was frozen, overwhelmed by the sheer power radiating from the entity. But then, she remembered her purpose, her responsibility. She, the bearer of the obsidian heart, was the only hope for Eldoria.

With renewed resolve, Seraphina raised her hand, the darkness within her coalescing into a swirling ball of power. This wasn't about destroying the entity, for darkness could not be truly eradicated. But it could be contained, pushed back.

Channeling the obsidian heart with all her might, Seraphina hurled the ball of concentrated darkness at the swirling vortex. It struck true, momentarily disrupting the entity's pulsating rhythm. A wave of shock reverberated through the cavern, the whispers morphing into a horrified screech.

The entity, for the first time, seemed to react. It pulsed with renewed fury, tendrils of darkness lashing out at Seraphina. She dodged with a roll, a surge of adrenaline coursing through her veins. This was it. The moment of truth.

She knew brute force wouldn't be enough. She needed to understand the entity, its purpose, its essence. Closing her eyes, she focused on the obsidian heart within, extending a tendril of her own darkness towards the entity.

It was like dipping a toe into a churning sea of chaos. Images flashed through her mind – a primal emptiness, a yearning for oblivion, a desperate struggle against the encroaching light. It was a being of pure negativity, driven by an insatiable hunger to consume all light and life.

But within the chaos, Seraphina sensed a flicker of something else – a loneliness, an isolation that mirrored her own ostracized past. It was a twisted reflection, but a reflection nonetheless.

Opening her eyes, Seraphina didn't attack. Instead, she spoke, her voice echoing through the cavern. "You are not alone," she declared. "Darkness is a part of everything, even light. There is no escaping it."

The entity pulsed in response, a confused, almost questioning hum resonating through the chamber. Seraphina pressed on. "But you don't have to consume everything," she continued. "There can be balance. Darkness can exist alongside light, each nurturing the other."

The cavern fell silent, even the whispers holding their breath. The entity, for the first time, seemed to hesitate, the red glow dimming slightly.

Taking a deep breath, Seraphina held out her hand, the darkness within her shimmering faintly. "Let's coexist," she offered. "Eldoria deserves a balance, not just light, but not just darkness either."

The cavern grew even quieter, the tension thick enough to cut with a knife. Then, slowly, cautiously, the entity reciprocated. A tendril of its own darkness reached out, connecting with Seraphina's. It was a tentative connection, a fragile bridge between light and dark.

A wave of relief washed over Seraphina. She hadn't destroyed the Shadowbane, but she had achieved something more significant – an understanding. Darkness wasn't the enemy; it was a force of nature, just like light. The key was not to eradicate it, but to find a way to coexist.

The pulsating heart within the cavern began to slow, the red glow softening into a deep purple. The whispers, once a cacophony of torment, morphed into a low, mournful hum. The Shadowbane wasn't disappearing, but it was receding, its hold on Eldoria loosening.

With a final, grateful thrum, the entity retracted its tendril. Seraphina felt a surge of exhaustion, the adrenaline leaving her system. The battle was over, not with a bang, but with a whisper of understanding.

As the dust settled, Seraphina knew her journey wasn't over. She needed to return to Eldoria, share what she had learned, and help the world find a way to live in harmony with the darkness. But for now, in the heart of Shadowfell, a fragile peace had been established, a testament to the power of understanding, even in the face of overwhelming darkness.

The return journey from Shadowfell felt lighter, almost buoyant. The whispers, once a constant torment, now seemed like a distant echo. Seraphina emerged from the swirling vortex onto the desolate plateau, the faint twilight sky a welcome sight.

But the elation of victory was tinged with a profound sense of responsibility. The world wouldn't change overnight. She had achieved a fragile peace within the heart of Shadowfell, but convincing the people of Eldoria to embrace darkness alongside light would be a far greater challenge.

As she began her descent back down the treacherous mountain range, a flicker of movement on the horizon caught her eye. A lone figure, cloaked in black robes, stood silhouetted against the twilight sky. It was the same figure who had warned her at the ruins, the one who spoke of the Shadowbane's power.

Seraphina approached cautiously, unsure of the figure's intentions. As she drew closer, the figure turned, revealing a face etched with age and weariness, yet tinged with a glimmer of curiosity.

"You have returned," the figure rasped, its voice dry and ancient. "And not as I expected."

Seraphina stopped a few paces away. "I did not destroy the Shadowbane," she admitted. "But I found a different way."

The figure raised an eyebrow, a flicker of surprise crossing its face. "Tell me," it invited, gesturing towards a nearby rock formation.

Seraphina recounted the events within the heart of Shadowfell – her confrontation with the entity, the tentative bridge she built with her own darkness, the fragile peace that had been established. The figure listened intently, its silence a stark contrast to the ever-present whispers.

As Seraphina finished, a long silence fell between them. Finally, the figure spoke, its voice infused with a newfound respect. "You achieved the impossible, child. You found a way to coexist with darkness."

"It wasn't easy," Seraphina confessed, "but it was the only way."

The figure nodded slowly. "Perhaps," it mused. "There is wisdom in your words, child. More wisdom than many in Eldoria possess."

A flicker of hope ignited within Seraphina. Maybe, just maybe, the people of Eldoria would be receptive to her message. "What can I do now?" she asked, her voice full of conviction.

The figure smiled faintly, a rare sight on its weathered face. "Return to Eldoria, child," it said. "Tell them your story. Show them that darkness is not their enemy, but a part of their world. You may not be met with open arms, but you have planted a seed. And with time, nurture, and a little courage, it may just blossom into a future where light and darkness exist in harmony."

Seraphina took a deep breath, the weight of the world seemingly lighter on her shoulders. This wasn't a victory march, but the beginning of a long journey. Yet, she was no longer alone. She carried within her the knowledge gleaned from Shadowfell, the power of the obsidian heart, and a newfound confidence.

With a nod of thanks to the enigmatic figure, Seraphina turned towards the distant horizon, where Eldoria awaited. The path ahead wouldn't be easy, but Seraphina, the girl who once ostracized for the darkness within, now embraced it. She was ready to face her people, not as a harbinger of doom, but as a beacon of hope, a testament to the power of understanding, and the possibility of a world bathed in both light and darkness.

The journey back to Eldoria felt different. Gone were the gnawing fear and crushing isolation. In their place, a steely resolve burned within Seraphina. She wasn't just returning as a warrior who had confronted the heart of Shadowfell; she was returning as a bridge, a testament to the possibility of coexistence.

As she neared the familiar borders of her village, a wave of apprehension washed over her. The villagers' fearful faces flashed before her eyes, their whispers of the cursed child echoing in her mind. Yet, this time, she wouldn't shy away.

The village gates stood ajar, a stark contrast to the fortified stance they had taken during her departure. Hesitantly, Seraphina stepped through, the sound of her footsteps echoing across the deserted square.

Suddenly, a voice boomed from behind a building. "Seraphina! Is that truly you?"

Elara emerged from the shadows, her face etched with a mixture of disbelief and relief. The sight of her childhood friend, the one who had always believed in her, brought a wave of warmth to Seraphina's chest.

They embraced tightly, the years of separation melting away in the comfort of their friendship. Elara, filled with questions, listened intently as Seraphina recounted her journey – the descent into Shadowfell, the confrontation with the entity, and the fragile peace that had been established.

Elara's eyes widened with each revelation. "You didn't destroy it?" she breathed, finally.

Seraphina shook her head. "No," she admitted. "Darkness cannot be eradicated. But it can be understood. It can coexist with light."

Elara pondered this for a moment, her brow furrowed in thought. "It sounds...impossible," she confessed. "But then again, no one thought you could even reach the heart of Shadowfell, let alone return alive."

Seraphina smiled faintly. "Things are possible, Elara, even the seemingly impossible. It all depends on our perspective."

Elara returned the smile, a hint of hope flickering in her eyes. "Then spread this new perspective, Seraphina. We need to hear it. Eldoria needs to hear it."

Spreading the message wouldn't be easy. Deep-seated fear wasn't easily quelled. But with Elara by her side, Seraphina decided to summon the village council.

The council chamber buzzed with nervous energy as Seraphina stood before them. The fear in their eyes was palpable, but so was a flicker of curiosity. With a deep breath, Seraphina launched into her tale, weaving a narrative of hardship, understanding, and ultimately, a fragile peace.

As she spoke, the room fell silent. The whispers of a "cursed child" were replaced by the rustle of shifting clothes and the occasional gasp of surprise. When she finished, a long silence hung heavy in the air.

Finally, the eldest council member, a man weathered by time and worry, spoke. "This is a radical notion, child," he said, his voice raspy. "Can we truly trust darkness?"

Seraphina met his gaze with unwavering resolve. "Darkness isn't a monster," she said. "It's a part of nature, just like light. The key isn't to eradicate it, but to find a way to live in harmony with it."

The council members exchanged glances, their faces etched with skepticism. But the seed of doubt had been planted. The fear of the unknown no longer held the same power when confronted with a story of understanding and possibility.

In the days that followed, Seraphina spoke to the village elders, the farmers, the children – anyone who would listen. She shared her experiences, not as an indictment of their past fears, but as a call to consider a new future.

Acceptance was slow and filled with apprehension. Yet, with each person who listened, a tiny shift occurred. The whispers of a "cursed child" morphed into murmured discussions of a brave warrior, a bearer of a strange but potentially hopeful message.

The journey to a world where light and darkness lived in harmony wouldn't be easy. It would take time, education, and a constant effort to bridge the gap of fear. But for the first time, Seraphina saw the flicker of a shared dream – a world bathed in both light and darkness, a world where the girl once ostracized for her darkness had become a beacon of hope for a future bathed in both.

News of Seraphina's return and her message of coexistence with darkness spread like wildfire through Eldoria. Some villages embraced her narrative with open arms, relieved to have a glimmer of hope after years of fear. Others, however, clung to their ingrained fear of the Shadowbane, dismissing Seraphina's story as fantasy or a dangerous delusion.

Eldoria's capital city, Lumina, became the battleground for these two opposing viewpoints. The city, once a bastion of light, now wrestled with an uncomfortable truth - that darkness wasn't simply their enemy, but a fundamental force intertwined with their very existence.

Seraphina, with Elara by her side, found herself thrust into the political maelstrom. The Luminari Council, the governing body of Eldoria, was deeply divided. The staunch traditionalists, led by Archmage Theon, advocated for a renewed offensive against the Shadowbane, refusing to believe Seraphina's claims.

However, a new faction emerged within the council. Led by the young and visionary Councilwoman Anya, they saw promise in Seraphina's message. They believed that understanding the darkness could be the key to breaking the cycle of fear and destruction.

The council chamber became a stage for heated debates. Theon, his voice laced with righteous fury, thundered: "Coexistence with darkness? What madness is this? Darkness seeks only to consume! We must eradicate it!"

Anya, in turn, countered with calm conviction: "For centuries, we've fought the darkness, and it only grows stronger. Perhaps Seraphina offers a new way. A way to live in harmony with both light and shadow."

Seraphina, once ostracized and shunned, now stood at the center of this battle of ideologies. She spoke not as a warrior, but as an ambassador, bridging the gap between fear and understanding.

She recounted her journey, not focusing on the horrors of Shadowfell, but on the entity within its heart. It wasn't a mindless monster, but a force of nature, seeking not conquest, but simply a place to exist.

Her words resonated with some, particularly the younger generation who hadn't known a world free of the Shadowbane's influence. But for those hardened by years of fear, her story seemed too outlandish to believe.

The Luminari Council remained deadlocked. Days turned into weeks, the debate growing more heated with each passing session. Finally, Anya proposed a compromise.

"Let us send a delegation to the heart of Shadowfell," she declared. "Let them see the truth for themselves."

This proposal ignited a fresh wave of arguments. Theon vehemently opposed it, fearing such a journey was a fool's errand. But Anya, with unwavering determination, pressed her point.

"Fear thrives in the dark," she argued. "Let us shed light on the unknown and see what we truly face."

After hours of deliberation, the council reached a precarious decision. A small delegation, led by Anya and accompanied by Seraphina, would journey to Shadowfell. It was a risky gamble, a chance encounter that could either pave the way for peace or unleash unimaginable consequences.

As the preparations for the journey were underway, a strange calm settled over Eldoria. People watched with bated breath, their hearts filled with a mixture of anxiety and a newly awakened hope. The fate of Eldoria, once balanced on a knife's edge, now rested on the shoulders of a young woman who once embraced her darkness and an ambassador who dared to bridge the gap between light and shadow.

Their journey to Shadowfell, fraught with danger and uncertainty, would decide whether Eldoria could truly embrace a future bathed in both light and darkness.

About the Author

Mrigendra Bharti, born on June 29, 2004, in South Delhi, India, is a multifaceted individual recognized as the owner of Mrigendra Bharti Group InfoTech India Co. Pvt Ltd. Beyond his entrepreneurial endeavors, he is a distinguished music producer, director, and a budding writer.

Embarking on his professional journey at a young age, Mrigendra Bharti's visionary leadership has led to the establishment of several successful ventures, including Croma Music Series Entertainment, Sellbrochure, Fauget Innovative, and more.

What sets Mrigendra apart is his early initiation into the world of business. His foray into the unknown realms of entrepreneurship began during his 10th-grade years, where he delved into the music industry. This initial venture laid the foundation for subsequent achievements, showcasing his dedication and resilience.

Having honed his skills in music, Mrigendra Bharti not only demonstrated significant growth in his craft but also expanded his professional network. His passion extends beyond music, encompassing app and website development, as well as graphic design.

Fueled by his creative aspirations, Mrigendra established the Mrigendra Bharti Group, a company specializing in website and app development. Currently, he collaborates with a dedicated team, collectively working on ambitious projects that promise innovation and excellence.

Mrigendra's journey serves as an inspiration, particularly for today's students, highlighting the potential of youthful determination and the ability to transform innovative ideas into successful businesses. As he continues to make strides in various domains, Mrigendra Bharti remains a dynamic force, contributing vibrancy to the realms of business, music, and technology.

Read more at https://www.imwriter-mrigendra.rf.gd.